First published in Great Britain in 1993
by Simon & Schuster Young Books
Campus 400
Maylands Avenue
Hemel Hempstead
Herts HP2 7EZ

Reprinted 1993, 1994

Text © 1993 Christine Pullein-Thompson
Illustrations © 1993 Gilly Marklew

The right of Christine Pullein-Thompson to be identified as the author of this
Work and the right of Gilly Marklew to be identified as the illustrator of this
Work has been asserted to them in accordance with the Copyright, Designs and
Patents Act 1988.

Typeset in 16/24pt Garamond by Goodfellow & Egan Ltd, Cambridge
Printed and bound in Portugal by Edições ASA

British Library Cataloguing in Publication Data available

ISBN 0 7500 1361 3
ISBN 0 7500 1362 1 (pbk)

Christine Pullein-Thompson

I Want That PONY!

Illustrated by Gilly Marklew

SIMON & SCHUSTER
YOUNG BOOKS

Chapter One

"I want that pony down the road," said Sophy.

"But that pony belongs to someone else," said Dad.

No one knew why Sophy wanted a pony so much. Mum said it was as though she had suddenly caught something like measles. Dad said that she would grow out of it. But Sophy knew that she would never grow out of it.

She was tired of her toys. She didn't really want to see her friends any more – there was only one thing she wanted and that was Flash, the brown pony with rather a small eye, and large ears, and white on his face who lived only a few metres away down the Close.

Sophy was always hanging over the field gate feeding Flash. Apples and carrots vanished from the larder as though they had a houseful of mice, and Mum had stopped buying lump sugar altogether.

Sometimes Sophy dreamt that she was riding Flash. In her dreams, she simply climbed on to him and – hey presto – she could ride!

But Flash didn't belong to Sophy: he belonged to Alison. And Alison loved Flash too.

Three times she asked Sophy to stop feeding him.

"Lumps of sugar are bad for his teeth," she said.

"I'll only give him carrots, then," replied Sophy.

"He'll choke on carrots unless they're sliced," said Alison scowling. "Anyway he's not your pony – he's mine."

Sophy had no answer to that, but from then on she sliced the carrots she took to Flash.

Watching Sophy slicing carrots, Mum said, "Do you have to feed him all my carrots? He's fat enough as it is."

"But he expects them now," said Sophy obstinately. "He's always waiting for them, Mum."

Mum and Dad were becoming worried, for Sophy seemed bewitched by Flash and they were not sure what to do. Then Dad brought home a kitten, hoping that it would take Sophy's mind off Flash.

"There you are, it's yours," he said, handing the kitten to her. "But don't give him carrots, will you?" And they both laughed.

Sophy named the kitten Tabby because it was a tabby. But much as Sophy loved Tabby, he wasn't Flash. And you can't *ride* a cat.

12

Then Mum had an even better idea. She bought Sophy a red bike; it wasn't new, but it had a bell, and a little basket attached to the handlebars.

"There, you can ride that," she said, hugging Sophy.

Sophy soon learnt to ride the bike up and down the Close. She did like it, but not as much as Flash, because you can't pat a bike's neck and it doesn't whinny when it sees you coming and blow warm breath down your neck.

So now, twice a day, Sophy filled the little
basket on the bike with goodies for Flash and
rode it to his field. She went first thing in the
morning and every day after tea, wet or fine.

Alison watched her from an upstairs window in her house and grew angrier and angrier. She tried to tell her parents about Sophy, but they told her not to be selfish, and to share her pony with her friends. But Sophy wasn't Alison's friend, and Alison didn't see why she should share her pony with someone she didn't even like.

Chapter Two

Sophy's mum telephoned Alison's mum several times to discuss Sophy's visits to Flash, but she was never in. Sophy's mum wanted to ask whether it was all right for Sophy to feed Flash, because she didn't want Sophy to be a nuisance.

Meanwhile, Alison was growing crosser and crosser for, whenever she looked for Flash, he was always standing with his head hanging over the field gate waiting for Sophy to appear on her little red bike.

Flash didn't like Alison as much as Sophy, because Alison often rode him for hours on end, and Flash didn't like work – he would far rather stand with his head over the gate waiting for Sophy.

Then one day Alison had a brainwave. She decided to teach Sophy a lesson. So the next time she saw Sophy, she called out, "Come tomorrow evening in trousers and then you can ride Flash. Okay?"

"Really and truly?" cried Sophy surprised.

"Yes, really and truly," replied Alison. "But don't tell your parents. I'll lend you my hat. Riding is eesy peesy."

"Thank you, thank you very much," said Sophy in her politest voice, riding away on her bike, feeling as though her head was high in the clouds, because she was so happy.

Sophy felt bad about not telling Mum and Dad about the promised ride; usually she told them everything. She knew it was wrong not to tell them, but she wanted to ride Flash so much that she told herself it didn't matter – not this time.

Mum and Dad were still worrying about Sophy, who was too excited to eat much tea that day and wouldn't tell them why.

Mum was looking forward to the winter now. "She won't want to see Flash when it's teeming with rain," she said.

"Perhaps they'll keep him locked in the stable in the winter," said Dad hopefully.

"I wish she had never set eyes on the pony," said Mum.

"Soon school will start again," said Dad.

Sophy hardly slept that night. And when she did doze off, she dreamt that Alison turned into a witch and changed Flash into a broomstick and flew off on him.

23

Sophy was too excited to eat much breakfast. Mum and Dad looked at one another. It was getting beyond a joke, they said. Something would have to be done.

Sophy imagined herself riding Flash. Alison had said it was eesy peesy.

"In a few days you'll
have a lovely surprise,"
she said.

"What sort of surprise?"
asked Mum warily.

"Just a lovely one," said Sophy.

"Where are you off to now?" asked Dad a
moment later.

"Just to see Flash. I'll be back soon,"
replied Sophy, her eyes shining.

Sophy sang as she rode her little red bike
along the Close. In a few days I'll be able to
ride a pony. Then won't Mum and Dad be
surprised, she thought. She had put on her
best trousers and a T-shirt.

Flash wasn't waiting by the gate. Alison
was grooming him by a little stable at the far
end of the field. She waved and called,
"Come over. We're nearly ready for you."
Flash raised his head and whinnied.

"Leave your titbits behind,
Sophy. Keep them for later,"
called Alison, feeling jealous.

Soon Sophy was patting Flash. "It's very kind of you to let me ride him," she said politely. "I've never ridden properly before, or only on the beach and at fêtes."

Alison smiled and it wasn't a nice smile.

Then she helped Sophy up on to Flash. She
pulled up the stirrups, put her hat on Sophy's
head and gave her the reins to hold.

Sophy felt like a princess sitting on Flash.
She wished now that Mum and Dad were
there to see her.

"I will lead you a little way and then you can ride on your own," said Alison.

She led Flash right round the field. Flash didn't want to go anywhere. He wanted to be in the stable munching hay, or waiting for Sophy by the gate. He put his ears back and walked more and more slowly. Alison stopped him by the stable.

"Well done," she said. "Now give him a good kick with your heels and gallop to the end of the field and back."

"But I can't gallop," cried Sophy.

"Trot then," said Alison.

Alison knew what Flash would do. He had done it to most of her friends, but they had never been hurt. Afterwards they always said, "Oh Alison, how do *you* make him do what he's told? You must be a very good rider." And that always pleased Alison.

31

So now Sophy gave Flash a frightened little kick with her heels and the pony set off down the field quite fast, with Sophy holding on to the saddle with both hands. But after only a little way, Flash gave a tiny buck, swung round and raced back towards the stable.

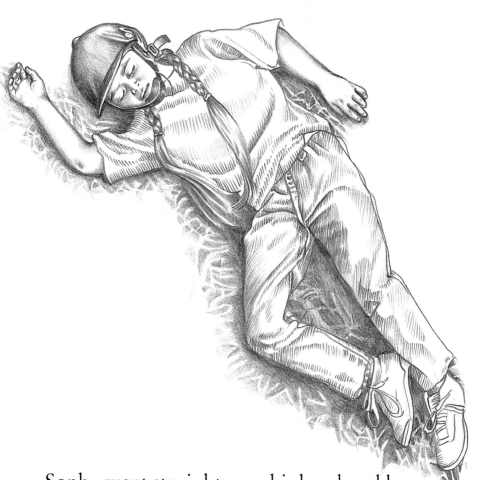

Sophy went straight over his head and lay
in the grass groaning. She wasn't really hurt,
but inside she was hurting at the thought that
she couldn't ride after all. And also because
Flash, whom she loved, had let her down and,
leaving her lying in the grass, had gone
straight back to Alison and his stable.

And now Alison, who had thought Sophy
would jump up straight away like her friends
always did, was scared. She called, "Are you
all right, Sophy? Are you hurt?"

But Sophy wouldn't answer because she
felt angry and let down by both Alison *and*
Flash, and she wanted them to think she was
dead.

Chapter Three

Sophy's mum was walking towards the field, wondering why Sophy had been so long. She arrived just in time to see Sophy falling off.

She leapt over the gate and ran to Sophy.

"Sophy, are you all right?" she cried.

Sophy slowly picked herself up, and then Mum turned to Alison and said, "You're a wicked girl letting Sophy ride by herself, and I shall be having words with your mother. And as for you, Sophy . . ."

"It wasn't my fault," said Alison beginning to cry.

"She told me to gallop," said Sophy.

"You're coming straight home," replied Mum. "I'm very cross with both of you; you could have been badly hurt, Sophy."

"But I'm fine," said Sophy, mounting her bike and looking sadly at the titbits in the basket which she had meant to give Flash.

Then she said, "But Flash was horrid, Mum. He threw me off on purpose. He knew I couldn't ride. And I've given him so many nice things to eat. I thought he loved me, Mum."

When they reached home, Mum sent Sophy straight to her room, and then she rang up Alison's mother and told her exactly what had happened.

Alison's mother was angry too. But soon she explained that Sophy's titbits were making Flash naughtier and naughtier, so that sometimes when Alison wanted to ride him in the woods nearby, he refused to go any further than the gate.

Later Alison's mum appeared at the front door with a box of chocolates and some flowers. "These are from Alison. She's very sorry. If only she had told me what was happening, I would have sorted it out weeks ago," she said.

"I don't know what to say," replied Mum. "Sophy's thought of nothing but Flash for weeks and weeks now. We got her a kitten, and a bike, but it didn't make any difference. And now she's crying her eyes out upstairs."

"I expect she thought of him as a sort of toy," said Alison's mum.

"But ponies are living creatures, and I'm still very angry with Alison because she knows full well how naughty Flash can be."

That evening, Mum and Dad talked to
Sophy for a long time. They said that she
should never have ridden without one of
them being there and they explained that you
can't just learn to ride a pony like you learn
to ride a bike. "It takes years," said Dad.

"And you need a proper teacher, like at school," added Mum.

"Someone who understands ponies, not a kid like Alison," said Dad.

"But now we're going to pay for you to have riding lessons," said Mum.

"And in exchange you must leave Flash alone," added Dad. "All right?"

"I don't mind about Flash, because I know he doesn't really love me," said Sophy slowly. "But when can I start the lessons?"

"The day after tomorrow. But we'll have to buy you a proper riding hat first," replied Dad.

"And jodphurs, and boots," said Mum.

Sophy picked up Tabby and cuddled him. Riding Flash had been just a silly dream – she knew that now. But the day after tomorrow would be different; it would be real.

"You've booked the lessons, haven't you?"
she asked, just to be sure.

"Yes, it's all fixed up, and you're going to
ride a lovely pony called Melody," said
Mum.

That night, when Sophy fell asleep, she dreamt she was riding through the air on a beautiful flying horse, and this time she could really ride!

Look out for other exciting new titles in the **Storybooks** series.

Babybug
Catherine Storr
Illustrated by Fiona Dunbar

When Tania's new baby brother arrives, she can't understand what all the fuss is about. He even has a baby alarm, so her parents can hear him crying when he's in another room! Then Tania has a wonderful idea – why not switch the alarm around so she can hear what her parents say when she's not in the room?

The Shoemaker's Boy
Joan Aiken
Illustrated by Alan Marks

When his father goes off on a pilgrimage, Jem is left in charge of the shoemaker's shop. This proves a bigger task than Jem had realised!

T.V. Genie
John Talbot

Paul isn't looking forward to staying with his grandad over the holidays. But he changes his mind when he discovers an old television set up in the attic. It's got black and white magic!

Seymour Finds a Home
Dyan Sheldon
Illustrated by Nigel McMullen

Seymour is a dragon with a problem. Whenever he tries to breathe fire, all that comes out is snow!

You can buy all these books from your local bookshop, or they can be ordered direct from the publishers. For more information about Storybooks write to The Sales Department, Simon & Schuster Young Books, Campus 400, Maylands Avenue, Hemel Hempstead HP2 7EZ.